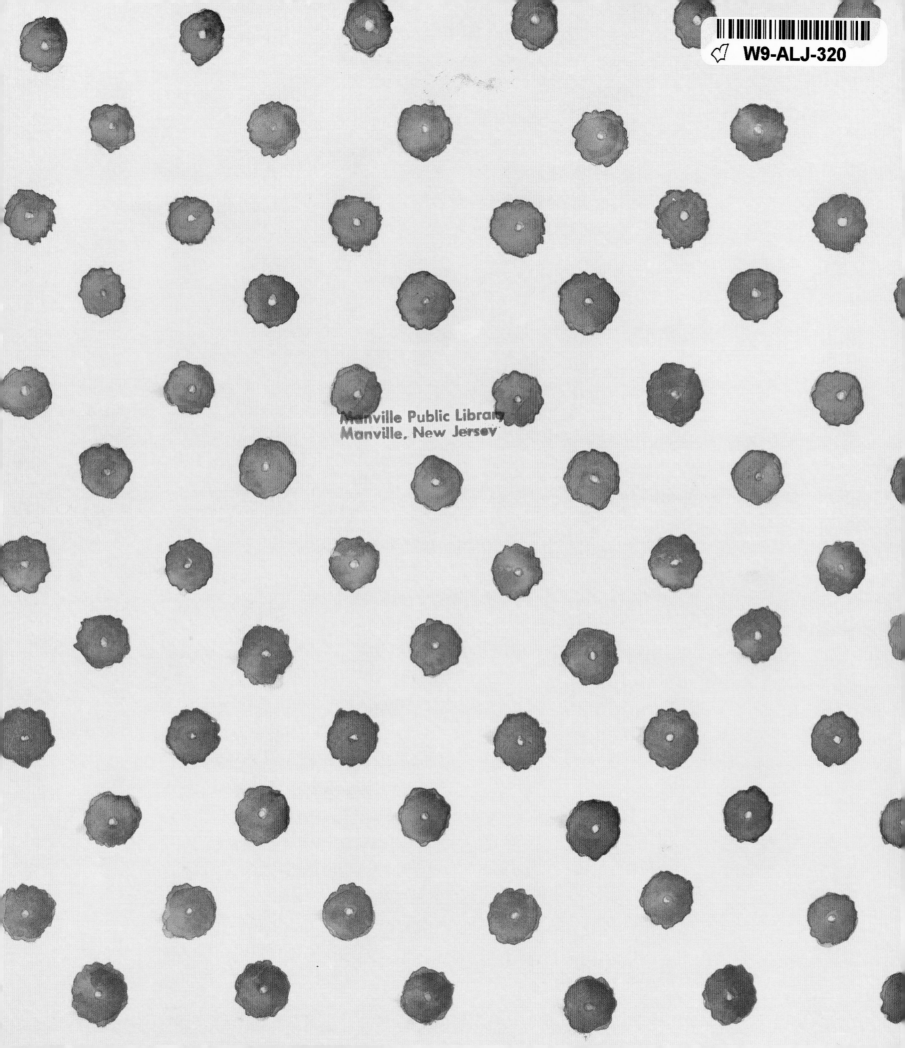

Whose Garden Is It?

MARY ANN HOBERMAN

ILLUSTRATED BY JANE DYER

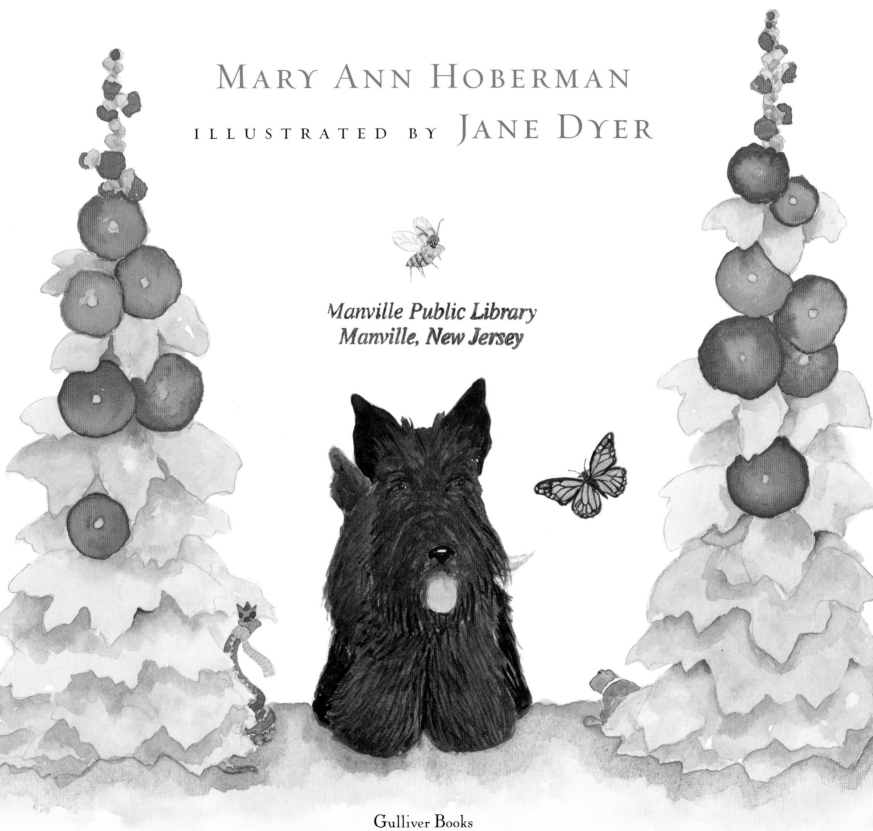

Gulliver Books

Harcourt, Inc.

Orlando Austin New York San Diego Toronto London

www.HarcourtBooks.com

Library of Congress Cataloging-in-Publication Data
Hoberman, Mary Ann.
Whose garden is it?/by Mary Ann Hoberman; illustrated by Jane Dyer.
p. cm.
"Gulliver Books."
Summary: When Mrs. McGee walks through a garden wondering whose it is, all of the plants and animals
as well as the sun and the gardener claim it as their own.
[1. Gardens—Fiction. 2. Stories in rhyme.] I. Dyer, Jane, ill. II. Title.
PZ8.3.H66Wk 2004
[E]—dc21   99-50705
ISBN 0-15-202631-2

First edition

A C E G H F D B

Printed in Singapore

The illustrations in this book were done in Holbein watercolors
on Waterford 140 lb. hot-press watercolor paper.
The display type was set in OptiDeligne.
The text type was set in Powhatten.
Color separations by Bright Arts Ltd., Hong Kong
Printed and bound by Tien Wah Press, Singapore
This book was printed on totally chlorine-free Stora Enso Matte paper.
Production supervision by Sandra Grebenar and Ginger Boyer
Designed by Lydia D'moch

Once again to Norm, beloved partner in the garden
—M. A. H.

For Tom, who plants the gardens, with love
—J. D.

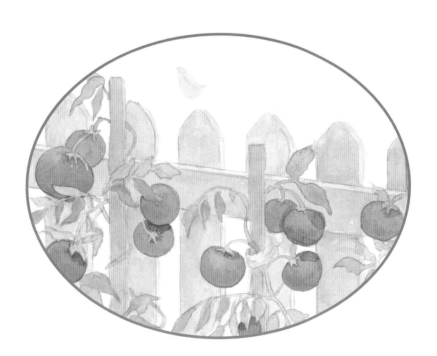

Mrs. McGee went out walking one day,
And as she was cheerfully wending her way,
She passed by a garden with colors so bright.
She never had seen such a beautiful sight!
    "How splendid! How pleasant! How simply exquisite!
    This garden is perfect...
    But whose garden is it?"

The gardener answered, "It's clear as can be!
This garden you see belongs only to me!
I am the owner and everyone knows it.
I am the person who plants it and grows it.
See how I keep it in first-rate condition?
No one can come here without my permission."

The gardener bowed and allowed her to pass,

Then went back to weeding, and seeding the grass.

He grumbled to see that some lettuce was gone

And stamped on some strange bumpy lumps in the lawn.

Then Mrs. McGee heard a sharp little squeak.

Up popped a rabbit, who started to speak.

"He says it is his, but I cannot agree!

If no one can come here, then what about me?

I've lived my whole life here. Just see how I dine!

He grows me my dinner! This garden is mine!"

"Not so!" sniffed the woodchuck from under a wall.
"You eat just a little, but I eat it all!
I gobble each bud and each leaf and each vine!
I eat the whole garden! This garden is mine!"

"It's mine!" the bird twittered from high in a tree.
"The worms in the garden were put there for me!"

"Not so!" sighed the worm. "Why, I make the soil fine,
And that's why I'm put here. This garden is mine!"

"It's mine," the wasp grumbled. "I've built a fine nest here."
"It's mine," buzzed the honeybee. "You're just a pest here.
I pollinate flowers. It's easy to see
This garden would not even *be* without me!"

"Or me!" bragged the butterfly. "Begging your pardon,
I, too, spread the pollen all over this garden."

"It's mine!" squeaked the squash bug.
"No, mine!" whined the flea.
"No, mine!" snapped the beetle. "It's planted for me!"

"Not so!" the snake hissed from down under a pine.
"I feast on you fellows! This garden is mine!"

"It's mine," groaned the mole. "It is full of my furrows."

"It's mine," squealed the vole. "See my bumps and my burrows."

The toads and the turtles, the squirrels and hares,
The chipmunks and crickets—all claimed it was theirs.

Then Mrs. McGee heard a hum in her ear.
Who was that calling her? What did she hear?

"It is mine," a plant rustled. "I blossom in season.
If this is a garden, then I am the reason."

"No, mine," a weed whistled, awave in the breeze.
"You have to be planted. I grow where I please."

"It is mine," breathed the soil. "That is perfectly clear.
Nothing could grow here if I were not here."
"It is mine," barked the tree, "for I shelter and shade you.
And as my leaves fall, year by year I have made you."

"It is mine," smiled the sun, shining down on the tree.
"I bring heat. I bring light. Nothing lives without me."

"Nothing lives without *me*! That is perfectly plain!
My showers bring flowers. It's mine!" cried the rain.

Then Mrs. McGee heard a faint little sound.
Something was murmuring under the ground.
Something that seemed as if she were quite near it.
Holding her breath, she bent over to hear it.

"It is mine," the seed whispered. "Although I am small,
I am the beginning, the start of it all.
The others may help me, but all of them know
Without me to grow from, no garden would grow."

The sun was now setting, the day growing late.
The gardener called as she walked out the gate,
"Now wasn't my garden a fine place to visit?"

But still she kept wondering
(Are *you* still wondering?),
Pondering,
Wondering,

Whose garden is it?